Luna's Odyssey: A Journey to Proxima Centauri b"?

1, Volume 1

Tiffany Tunis

Published by Tiffany Tunis, 2023.

This is a work of fiction. Similarities to real people, places, or events are entirely coincidental.

LUNA'S ODYSSEY: A JOURNEY TO PROXIMA CENTAURI B"?

First edition. November 26, 2023.

Written by Tiffany Tunis.

Chapter One: Luna's Last Day on Earth

Luna had always been fascinated by the stars. As a child, she would spend hours gazing up at the night sky, dreaming of the day she would finally get to see what lay beyond the confines of Earth. That day had finally arrived, but not in the way she had imagined.

It was the day of the big move. Luna's family was set to leave Earth and start a new life on Mars. The house was filled with a flurry of activity as everyone scrambled to get their belongings packed and ready for the journey. But Luna was not among them.

Instead, Luna was across town, saying her goodbyes to her friends. They had spent the day reminiscing about old times, sharing laughs, and promising to keep in touch. As the hours slipped by, Luna lost track of time. By the time she realized how late it was, it was already too late.

She rushed back home, her heart pounding in her chest. But as she arrived at the spaceport, she could only watch in despair as the ship carrying her family disappeared into the sky. She was too late.

In her panic, Luna did the only thing she could think of. She boarded the next available ship, praying that it was headed to Mars. But as the ship left Earth's atmosphere, Luna realized that she was not on a ship to Mars. She was on a ship to Proxima Centauri b, a distant exoplanet light-years away from her family.

As Luna stared out of the ship's window, watching Earth shrink into the distance, she felt a mix of fear and excitement. She was alone, on a ship to an unknown world. But as the initial shock wore off, Luna realized that she was embarking on the adventure she had always dreamed of.

And so, Luna's journey began. Not with a planned departure, but with a missed ship and an unexpected detour. Little did she know, this was just the beginning of her odyssey.

Chapter Two: The Unexpected Journey

As Luna settled into the ship, she couldn't help but feel a sense of awe. She was on a spaceship, traveling at light speed, headed towards a distant exoplanet. It was a far cry from the quiet suburban life she had known on Earth.

The ship was a marvel of technology, equipped with everything needed for long-duration space travel. There were living quarters, a mess hall, a medical bay, and even a recreation area. But what fascinated Luna the most was the ship's control room. It was here that the ship's crew navigated through the cosmos, their eyes always on the stars.

Luna spent her days exploring the ship, learning its ins and outs. She watched the crew as they worked, their movements precise and practiced. She listened to their conversations, their words filled with terms and jargon she didn't understand. But Luna was a quick learner. She asked questions, read manuals, and before long, she started understanding the workings of the ship.

But it wasn't all smooth sailing. Space travel was not without its challenges. There were times when the ship encountered cosmic storms, the turbulence causing the ship to shake violently. There were times when systems malfunctioned, causing panic among the crew. But through it all, Luna remained calm. She learned to trust in the crew, their skills honed through years of experience.

As the days turned into weeks, Luna found herself changing. She was no longer just a passenger on the ship; she was a part of the crew. She helped with repairs, assisted in navigating through asteroid fields, and even learned to operate some of the ship's systems. Luna was no longer the scared girl who had boarded the ship in a panic. She was becoming a space traveler.

And so, Luna's unexpected journey continued. With each passing day, she was getting further away from her family, but she was also getting closer to the stars she had always dreamed of. Little did she know, her journey was just beginning.

Chapter Three: First Glimpse of Proxima Centauri b

As Luna's ship journeyed through the cosmos, the days began to blend into one another. The constant hum of the ship's engines and the endless expanse of stars became her new normal. But everything changed the day Proxima Centauri b came into view.

Luna was in the control room when it happened. The crew had been preparing for this moment, their eyes glued to the monitors. And then, there it was. A small dot of light, growing larger and brighter with each passing second.

Proxima Centauri b was unlike anything Luna had ever seen. It was a world of vibrant colors and strange landscapes, its surface dotted with towering mountains and vast oceans. From the ship's window, Luna could see swirling clouds and patches of green, signs of an atmosphere and possible life.

The sight of Proxima Centauri b filled Luna with a sense of awe and wonder. She was about to set foot on an alien world, a place no human had ever been before. It was a moment Luna would remember for the rest of her life.

As the ship descended towards the planet, Luna could feel a mix of excitement and nervousness. She didn't know what awaited her on Proxima Centauri b, but she was ready to face it. After all, this was the adventure she had always dreamed of.

And so, Luna's journey continued. With her first glimpse of Proxima Centauri b, Luna was one step closer to her new home. But little did she know, her greatest adventures were yet to come.

Chapter Four: Life Aboard the Starship

Life aboard the starship was a far cry from Luna's life back on Earth. The confines of the ship became her world, the hum of the engines her constant companion. But Luna was not one to be deterred by her circumstances. She embraced her new life with an open mind and a thirst for knowledge.

The crew of the ship became Luna's new family. They were a diverse group, hailing from different parts of the galaxy, each with their own stories to tell. Luna spent her days learning from them, absorbing their knowledge and experiences.

She learned about the intricacies of interstellar navigation from the ship's pilot, a seasoned traveler with a wealth of experience. She learned about the various alien species they encountered from the ship's biologist, a woman with an insatiable curiosity for all forms of life. She learned about the ship's systems from the engineer, a man who could fix just about anything.

But it wasn't all work and no play. The crew knew how to keep their spirits high during the long journey. They would gather in the mess hall to share meals, swapping stories and laughter. They would play games to pass the time, with Luna often joining in.

As the weeks turned into months, Luna found herself changing. She was no longer the scared girl who had boarded the ship in a panic. She was becoming a part of the crew, her knowledge and skills growing with each passing day.

And so, Luna's journey continued. With each passing day, she was getting closer to Proxima Centauri b. But as she would soon discover, the real adventure was just beginning.

Chapter Five: Landing on the Alien Planet

The day Luna had been waiting for had finally arrived. The ship was about to land on Proxima Centauri b. Luna could hardly contain her excitement as she watched the alien planet grow larger in the ship's window.

The landing was a tense moment. The ship shuddered as it entered the planet's atmosphere, the heat shields glowing from the friction. But the crew was experienced and well-prepared. They expertly guided the ship through the descent, and soon, they were safely on the ground.

Luna's first steps on Proxima Centauri b were surreal. She was standing on an alien world, light-years away from Earth. The sky was a different color, the air smelled different, and even the gravity felt slightly off. But it was exhilarating. Luna was ready to start her new life on this strange, new world.

The first few days were a whirlwind of activity. Luna and the rest of the colonists were busy setting up their new homes and getting acclimated to their new environment. There were plants to be planted, systems to be set up, and a whole planet to explore.

Despite the hard work, Luna couldn't help but feel a sense of awe and wonder. Every day was a new adventure, filled with new discoveries and experiences. She was living her dream, exploring an alien world.

And so, Luna's journey continued. She may have landed on Proxima Centauri b, but her true journey was just beginning.

Chapter Six: Luna's New Home

As Luna stepped out of the ship and onto the surface of Proxima Centauri b, she felt a rush of exhilaration. She was standing on an alien world, a place no human had ever set foot before. The landscape was unlike anything she had ever seen, with towering alien trees reaching up to a sky that was a different hue from the one she was used to on Earth.

The first few days were spent setting up the colony. Luna and the other colonists worked tirelessly, constructing habitats, setting up communication systems, and starting the process of terraforming the land for agriculture. Despite the hard work, there was a sense of excitement and camaraderie among the colonists. They were pioneers, building a new life on a new world.

Luna's new home was a small habitat module, but she made it her own. She filled it with sketches of her observations, samples of alien flora, and a small terrarium with a few critters she had found on her explorations. It was small and humble, but it was hers.

In the evenings, Luna would often climb to the top of a nearby hill and look out at the colony. The sight of the habitats glowing softly against the alien landscape, the distant figures of her fellow colonists moving about, the strange constellations in the night sky - it was a constant reminder of how far she had come.

Despite the challenges and the homesickness, Luna found herself falling in love with Proxima Centauri b. She was captivated by its alien beauty, its untamed wilderness, its sense of mystery. It was not the home she had planned for, but it was the home she had found.

And so, Luna's journey continued. She was no longer just a passenger on a ship; she was a colonist, a pioneer, a resident of Proxima Centauri b.

And as she looked out at her new home, she knew that her adventure was just beginning.

Chapter Seven: Exploring the Colony

With their new homes established, the colonists began the task of building their community. Luna found herself in the heart of this endeavor. She was not just a resident of the colony; she was an active participant in its growth.

The colony was a blend of cultures and ideas, a melting pot of individuals from different corners of the galaxy. Luna found this diversity fascinating. She spent her days interacting with her fellow colonists, learning about their customs, their stories, and their dreams.

She helped set up the colony's communication systems, ensuring they could stay in touch with other colonies and Earth. She assisted in the construction of the research facility, where scientists would study Proxima Centauri b's unique ecosystem. She even helped establish the colony's first school, where she occasionally shared her knowledge and experiences with eager young minds.

But it was the exploration of Proxima Centauri b that Luna loved the most. Every day brought new discoveries. Alien flora and fauna, strange geological formations, even signs of ancient, long-gone civilizations. Luna documented all her findings, sharing them with the rest of the colony and the wider scientific community.

Life in the colony was not without its challenges. There were disagreements, resource shortages, and the ever-present danger of the unknown. But through it all, Luna remained optimistic. She believed in the colony and its potential. She believed in their shared dream of a new life on Proxima Centauri b.

And so, Luna's journey continued. She was not just a space traveler anymore; she was a pioneer, a colonist, a member of a growing community on an alien world. And as she looked out at the colony, she knew that she was exactly where she was meant to be.

Chapter Eight: Making New Friends

IN the midst of the bustling colony life, Luna found herself forming bonds with her fellow colonists. They were a diverse group, each with their own stories and experiences, but they all shared a common goal - to make Proxima Centauri b their new home.

There was Amara, the ship's pilot who had become Luna's mentor. Amara was a seasoned space traveler, her knowledge of the cosmos unparalleled. She taught Luna the intricacies of interstellar navigation, sharing stories of her own adventures along the way.

Then there was Jax, the colony's botanist. Jax had a deep love for all forms of life, his enthusiasm infectious. He took Luna under his wing, teaching her about the alien flora of Proxima Centauri b. Together, they cataloged new species, their findings contributing to the colony's growing knowledge of the planet.

And there was Kai, a young boy around Luna's age. Kai was a fellow Earthling, his family having joined the colony in the second wave of settlers. He shared Luna's sense of adventure, the two often embarking on explorations together.

These friendships became Luna's anchor in the alien world of Proxima Centauri b. They provided her with a sense of belonging, a reminder that she was not alone in this grand adventure. And in turn, Luna found herself opening up, sharing her own stories and experiences, her own hopes and dreams.

And so, Luna's journey continued. She was not just a colonist on an alien world; she was a friend, a mentor, a student. And as she looked out at the colony, her new friends by her side, she knew that she was home.

Chapter Nine: The Alien Ecosystem

As Luna settled into her new life on Proxima Centauri b, she found herself drawn to the planet's unique ecosystem. The alien world was teeming with life, its flora and fauna unlike anything she had seen on Earth.

There were towering trees with bioluminescent leaves, their soft glow illuminating the night. There were creatures that floated in the air, their bodies filled with a lighter-than-air gas. There were plants that moved on their own, their roots more like legs than anything else.

Luna spent her days exploring this alien ecosystem, her curiosity driving her to learn more. She worked closely with Jax, the colony's botanist, cataloging new species and studying their behaviors. Their findings were invaluable, contributing to the colony's understanding of the planet and its potential for colonization.

But it wasn't just the alien life that fascinated Luna. It was the way the ecosystem worked, the delicate balance that allowed life to flourish. She saw how every creature, every plant, played a role in the survival of the ecosystem. It was a complex web of life, each strand as important as the next.

This understanding deepened Luna's appreciation for Proxima Centauri b. She saw the planet not just as her new home, but as a living, breathing entity. She realized the importance of preserving this balance, of ensuring the survival of this alien ecosystem.

And so, Luna's journey continued. She was not just a colonist on an alien world; she was a steward, a guardian of an alien ecosystem. And as she looked out at the thriving life on Proxima Centauri b, she knew that she had a responsibility to protect it.

Chapter Ten: The Alien Artifact

One day, while exploring a remote part of Proxima Centauri b, Luna stumbled upon something extraordinary - an alien artifact. It was unlike anything she had ever seen, its design and material clearly not of human origin.

The artifact was a small device, its surface covered in strange symbols. Luna could not decipher them, but she knew they were important. She carefully collected the artifact, taking care not to damage it.

Back at the colony, the artifact caused quite a stir. The scientists were baffled, their instruments unable to determine the device's origin or purpose. But Luna was not deterred. She spent days, then weeks, studying the artifact, determined to unlock its secrets.

With the help of Amara and Jax, Luna began to decipher the symbols on the artifact. It was a slow process, filled with dead ends and false starts. But Luna was persistent. She knew that the artifact held the key to understanding the ancient civilization that once lived on Proxima Centauri b.

Finally, after weeks of hard work, Luna made a breakthrough. The symbols were not just random markings; they were a map. A map to a hidden city deep within the planet.

The discovery sent a wave of excitement through the colony. A hidden city could hold the answers to the many questions they had about the planet and its previous inhabitants. And Luna, the young girl who had accidentally boarded a ship to Proxima Centauri b, was at the center of it all.

And so, Luna's journey continued. She was not just a colonist on an alien world; she was an explorer, a discoverer of ancient secrets. And as she looked at the alien artifact, she knew that her greatest adventure was yet to come.

Chapter Eleven: Deciphering the Artifact

With the discovery of the alien artifact, Luna found herself at the heart of a new mystery. The artifact was a map to a hidden city, but deciphering it was no easy task. The symbols were unlike any language Luna had ever seen, their meanings elusive.

But Luna was not one to back down from a challenge. She threw herself into the task, spending long hours studying the artifact. She consulted with the colony's linguists and historians, delving into the ancient civilizations of the galaxy in search of clues.

Slowly, piece by piece, the map began to make sense. The symbols were not just random markings; they were a complex language, each symbol representing a specific location or direction. With this realization, Luna was able to start piecing together the route to the hidden city.

But the artifact held more than just a map. As Luna delved deeper, she discovered that it was also a key. A key that could unlock the city's ancient technology, technology that could change the course of human history.

The implications were staggering. The hidden city could hold the secrets to advanced energy production, faster-than-light travel, even immortality. The potential was limitless, and Luna found herself at the center of it all.

And so, Luna's journey continued. She was not just a colonist on an alien world; she was a key to a new future, a future that could change the course of human history. And as she looked at the alien artifact, she knew that her greatest adventure was yet to come.

Chapter Twelve: The Map to the Hidden City

With the alien artifact deciphered, Luna now had a map to the hidden city. It was located deep within the planet, in a region unexplored by the colonists. The journey would be dangerous, but Luna was ready. She had come too far to back down now.

Luna assembled a team of explorers, including Amara and Jax. They spent days preparing for the expedition, gathering supplies and mapping out their route. The excitement in the colony was palpable. They were on the brink of a major discovery, a discovery that could change everything.

The journey to the hidden city was fraught with challenges. They had to navigate through treacherous terrain, contend with alien wildlife, and overcome unexpected obstacles. But through it all, Luna and her team persevered. They were driven by a shared sense of purpose, a shared dream of discovery.

After weeks of travel, they finally arrived at the hidden city. It was a sight to behold, a sprawling metropolis of towering structures and advanced technology. It was clear that the city had been built by a civilization far more advanced than their own.

As Luna and her team explored the city, they made startling discoveries. They found advanced machinery, complex computer systems, even remnants of the city's inhabitants. It was a treasure trove of knowledge, a glimpse into a civilization that had reached the stars and beyond.

And so, Luna's journey continued. She was not just a colonist on an alien world; she was an explorer, a discoverer of ancient secrets. And as she stood in the heart of the hidden city, she knew that her greatest discoveries were yet to come.

Chapter Thirteen: Preparing for the Expedition

With the map to the hidden city in hand, Luna knew what she had to do next. She had to assemble a team and prepare for the expedition. It was a daunting task, but Luna was ready. She had come too far to back down now.

The first step was to assemble her team. Luna knew she couldn't do this alone. She needed a team of experts, individuals who were not only skilled but also shared her passion for discovery. She chose Amara for her piloting skills and knowledge of the cosmos, Jax for his expertise in alien flora and fauna, and a few other colonists who had shown a keen interest in her work.

Next, they needed to prepare for the journey. The hidden city was located in a remote and unexplored

Chapter Fourteen: The Journey to the Hidden City

With the team assembled and preparations complete, Luna and her team embarked on their journey to the hidden city. The journey was long and fraught with challenges. They had to navigate through treacherous terrains, face unpredictable weather, and even fend off alien creatures.

But through it all, Luna and her team persevered. They helped each other, worked together, and faced every challenge head-on. They were not just a team; they were a family, bound by a shared dream of discovery.

The first sight of the hidden city took their breath away. It was a sprawling metropolis, its towering structures a testament to the advanced civilization that once inhabited it. The city was eerily silent, its streets empty and buildings abandoned. But the sense of history was palpable. Every stone, every artifact, told a story of a civilization that had reached for the stars.

As Luna and her team stepped into the city, they knew they were walking in the footsteps of giants. They were standing on the threshold of a new era of discovery, ready to uncover the secrets of the ancient civilization.

And so, Luna's journey continued. She was not just a colonist on an alien world; she was an explorer, a pioneer, standing on the brink of a major discovery. And as she looked at the hidden city, she knew that her greatest adventure was yet to come.

Chapter Fifteen: Overcoming Obstacles

The hidden city was not easily accessible. Luna and her team had to overcome numerous obstacles to reach it. The city was located in a remote part of Proxima Centauri b, surrounded by treacherous terrain and guarded by strange, alien creatures.

But Luna was not deterred. She led her team with determination and courage, guiding them through the challenges that lay ahead. They climbed steep cliffs, navigated through dense forests, and crossed rushing rivers. They faced off against alien creatures, using their wits and resourcefulness to avoid conflict.

There were times when the challenges seemed insurmountable. There were times when they felt like giving up. But they pushed through, their shared goal driving them forward. They were not just a team; they were a family, their bonds strengthened by the trials they faced together.

After weeks of travel and countless challenges, they finally reached the hidden city. It was a moment of triumph, a testament to their perseverance and determination. They had done what no one else had done before - they had found the hidden city.

And so, Luna's journey continued. She was not just a colonist on an alien world; she was an explorer, a pioneer, standing on the threshold of a major discovery. And as she looked at the hidden city, she knew that her greatest adventure was yet to come.

Chapter Sixteen: Arrival at the Hidden City

After weeks of travel and overcoming numerous challenges, Luna and her team finally arrived at the hidden city. It was a moment of triumph, a testament to their determination and resilience. They had journeyed through uncharted territories, faced off against alien creatures, and now, they stood at the gates of an ancient city.

The city was a marvel of alien architecture, its structures towering high and stretching as far as the eye could see. It was clear that the city had been built by a civilization far more advanced than their own. The buildings were made of a material they had never seen before, shimmering in the alien sunlight.

As they ventured deeper into the city, they found it to be deserted. The once bustling metropolis was now eerily silent, its inhabitants long gone. But the city was not dead. It was filled with advanced technology, machines that hummed with energy, waiting to be awakened.

Luna and her team were in awe of their surroundings. They had discovered a piece of history, a testament to a civilization that had reached the stars. It was a humbling experience, a reminder of their place in the universe.

And so, Luna's journey continued. She was not just a colonist on an alien world; she was an explorer, a discoverer of ancient secrets. And as she stood in the heart of the hidden city, she knew that her greatest discoveries were yet to come.

Chapter Seventeen: Overcoming Obstacles

Exploring the hidden city was no easy task. The city was a maze of towering structures and winding streets, its layout unfamiliar and confusing. But Luna and her team were not deterred. They were explorers, ready to face whatever challenges came their way.

They encountered strange creatures, remnants of the city's past. They navigated through treacherous terrains, their path blocked by collapsed buildings and overgrown vegetation. They solved complex puzzles left behind by the city's ancient inhabitants, their solutions opening up new areas to explore.

But the biggest challenge was the city itself. The city was a relic of a bygone era, its systems old and deteriorating. Many of the city's machines were no longer functioning, their parts worn out from centuries of disuse. Restoring them required skill and ingenuity, a task that Luna and her team took on with determination.

Despite the challenges, Luna and her team made progress. They restored power to parts of the city, bringing ancient machines back to life. They deciphered more of the city's history, uncovering stories of its past. With each passing day, they were getting closer to uncovering the city's secrets.

And so, Luna's journey continued. She was not just a colonist on an alien world; she was an explorer, a pioneer, standing on the brink of a major discovery. And as she looked at the hidden city, she knew that her greatest adventure was yet to come.

Chapter Eighteen: Exploring the Alien City

With the hidden city now accessible, Luna and her team began their exploration. The city was a marvel of alien architecture, its structures unlike anything they had seen before. It was clear that the city had been built by a civilization far more advanced than their own.

As they ventured deeper into the city, they discovered more of its wonders. They found advanced machinery, complex computer systems, even remnants of the city's inhabitants. It was a treasure trove of knowledge, a glimpse into a civilization that had reached the stars and beyond.

But the city was not without its dangers. They encountered strange creatures, remnants of the city's past. They had to navigate through treacherous terrains, their path often blocked by collapsed buildings and overgrown vegetation. But through it all, Luna and her team persevered. They were explorers, ready to face whatever challenges came their way.

The exploration of the city was a slow process, but Luna was not in a hurry. She knew that the city held many secrets, and she was determined to uncover them all. With each passing day, they were getting closer to understanding the city and its ancient inhabitants.

And so, Luna's journey continued. She was not just a colonist on an alien world; she was an explorer, a discoverer of ancient secrets. And as she stood in the heart of the hidden city, she knew that her greatest discoveries were yet to come.

Chapter Nineteen: Uncovering Ancient Technology

As Luna and her team explored the hidden city, they made a startling discovery. The city was not just a relic of a bygone era; it was a treasure trove of ancient technology. Technology that was far more advanced than anything they had seen before.

They found machines that could manipulate matter, devices that could harness energy from the stars, even systems that could control the weather. It was clear that the city's inhabitants had been masters of technology, their knowledge far surpassing that of humanity.

But understanding this technology was no easy task. The machines were complex and their workings unfamiliar. But Luna was not deterred. She threw herself into the task, her curiosity driving her to learn more.

With the help of her team, Luna began to decipher the workings of the ancient technology. It was a slow process, filled with trial and error. But with each breakthrough, they were able to restore more of the city's systems, bringing the ancient city back to life.

The discovery of the ancient technology had profound implications. It opened up new possibilities for the colony, its potential applications limitless. Luna knew that they had only scratched the surface of what the city had to offer. And she was eager to uncover more of its secrets.

And so, Luna's journey continued. She was not just a colonist on an alien world; she was an explorer, a discoverer of ancient secrets. And as she delved deeper into the city's technology, she knew that her greatest discoveries were yet to come.

Chapter Twenty: Learning from the Ancients

The discovery of ancient technology was just the beginning. As Luna and her team delved deeper into the city, they uncovered more of its secrets. They found records of the city's history, its rise and fall, and the knowledge of its inhabitants.

The city's inhabitants had been a highly advanced civilization, their knowledge of science and technology far surpassing

Chapter Twenty-One: The City's Dark Secret

As Luna and her team delved deeper into the city's history, they uncovered a dark secret. The city's inhabitants had not just been advanced; they had been ambitious, their thirst for knowledge and power unquenchable.

They had harnessed the power of the stars, manipulated the fabric of space-time, even attempted to conquer death itself. But their ambition had been their downfall. They had triggered a catastrophe, a disaster of their own making that had led to their extinction.

The city was not just a testament to their achievements; it was a monument to their hubris. It was a sobering reminder of the dangers of unchecked ambition, of the consequences of playing with forces beyond their understanding.

But the city's dark secret was not a deterrent for Luna. Instead, it was a lesson. She realized that their knowledge and technology were not to blame; it was their misuse that had led to their downfall.

Luna vowed to learn from their mistakes. She would use their knowledge and technology for the betterment of the colony, to improve their lives and ensure their survival. She would ensure that their legacy would not be one of destruction, but of progress and prosperity.

And so, Luna's journey continued. She was not just a colonist on an alien world; she was a guardian of ancient knowledge, a steward of a powerful legacy. And as she stood in the heart of the hidden city, she knew that her greatest challenges were yet to come.

Chapter Twenty-Two: Sharing the Discoveries

With the secrets of the hidden city uncovered, Luna knew it was time to share her discoveries with the rest of the colony. She returned to the colony, her mind filled with the knowledge of the ancients and her heart heavy with the responsibility that came with it.

The colonists were in awe of Luna's discoveries. They marveled at the advanced technology, the complex systems, and the profound knowledge of the ancients. But they were also sobered by the city's dark secret, the cautionary tale of a civilization that had reached for the stars and fallen.

Luna shared her findings with the colony's leaders, the scientists, and the rest of the colonists. She spoke of the city's history, its rise and fall, and the lessons they could learn from it. She spoke of the potential of the ancient technology, the possibilities it opened up for the colony.

But Luna also spoke of the responsibility that came with this knowledge. She stressed the importance of using it wisely, of learning from the mistakes of the ancients. She spoke of the need for caution, for respect for the forces they were dealing with.

Her words resonated with the colonists. They understood the significance of Luna's discoveries and the responsibility that came with it. They pledged to use the knowledge for the betterment of the colony, to improve their lives and ensure their survival.

And so, Luna's journey continued. She was not just a colonist on an alien world; she was a beacon of knowledge, a guide for her fellow colonists. And as she looked out at the colony, her new home, she knew that her greatest achievements were yet to come.

Chapter Twenty-Three: Luna's New Role

With the discovery of the hidden city and the ancient technology, Luna found herself in a new role. She was no longer just a colonist; she was a leader, a guide, a beacon of knowledge for the rest of the colony.

Luna embraced her new role with grace and determination. She worked closely with the colony's scientists, sharing her knowledge and helping them understand the ancient technology. She guided the colonists in using the technology, ensuring it was used responsibly and for the benefit of all.

But Luna's new role was not without its challenges. There were disagreements, debates about the best way to use the technology. There were fears, concerns about the dangers of the ancient technology. But through it all, Luna remained steadfast. She listened to the concerns, addressed the fears, and guided the colony towards a future of progress and prosperity.

Luna's leadership had a profound impact on the colony. Under her guidance, the colony thrived. They harnessed the power of the ancient technology, improving their lives and ensuring their survival. They learned from the mistakes of the ancients, using their knowledge responsibly and with respect for the forces they were dealing with.

And so, Luna's journey continued. She was not just a colonist on an alien world; she was a leader, a guide, a beacon of knowledge. And as she looked out at the thriving colony, she knew that her greatest achievements were yet to come.

Chapter Twenty-Four: Advancements in Technology

With Luna's guidance, the colony began to harness the power of the ancient technology. They used it to improve their lives, to make their work easier, and to ensure their survival on Proxima Centauri b.

They used the technology to improve their communication systems, allowing them to stay in touch with other colonies and Earth. They used it to enhance their agricultural practices, increasing their food production and ensuring their sustainability. They used it to develop new energy sources, reducing their reliance on imported resources.

But the most significant advancement was in the field of medicine. The ancient technology allowed them to develop new treatments and cures, improving their health and increasing their lifespan. It was a breakthrough that had a profound impact on the colony, improving their quality of life and ensuring their survival.

Luna was at the heart of these advancements. She worked closely with the colony's scientists, guiding them in their research and helping them understand the ancient technology. Her knowledge and leadership were invaluable, driving the colony towards a future of progress and prosperity.

And so, Luna's journey continued. She was not just a colonist on an alien world; she was a pioneer, a leader, a beacon of progress. And as she looked out at the thriving colony, she knew that her greatest achievements were yet to come.

Chapter Twenty-Five: Recognition from the Scientific Community

Luna's discoveries did not go unnoticed. Word of the hidden city and the ancient technology reached the scientific community on Earth and other colonies. Luna's work was hailed as a major breakthrough, her discoveries opening up new avenues for research and development.

Luna was invited to speak at conferences, to share her findings with the scientific community. Despite her young age, Luna was recognized as a leading figure in the field of alien archaeology and technology. Her work was published in scientific journals, her discoveries studied by researchers across the galaxy.

But Luna remained humble. She knew that her discoveries were not her own, but the legacy of a civilization that had reached for the stars. She saw herself not as a pioneer, but as a steward of knowledge, a guardian of a powerful legacy.

Luna used her newfound recognition to advocate for responsible use of the ancient technology. She spoke of the need for caution, for respect for the forces they were dealing with. She spoke of the lessons they could learn from the ancients, the importance of using their knowledge for the benefit of all.

And so, Luna's journey continued. She was not just a colonist on an alien world; she was a beacon of knowledge, a guide for the scientific community. And as she stood on the stage, sharing her discoveries with the galaxy, she knew that her greatest achievements were yet to come.

Chapter Twenty-Six: Luna's Speech at the Intergalactic Conference

The day of the Intergalactic Conference finally arrived. Scientists and researchers from across the galaxy had gathered to hear Luna speak. As she stood on the stage, looking out at the sea of faces, Luna felt a mix of excitement and nervousness. But she was ready.

Luna spoke of her journey, of the missed ship and the unexpected detour that led her to Proxima Centauri b. She spoke of the hidden city, of the ancient technology, and of the civilization that had once thrived there. She spoke of the lessons they could learn from the ancients, of the importance of using their knowledge responsibly.

But most importantly, Luna spoke of the future. She spoke of the potential of the ancient technology, of the possibilities it opened up for humanity. She spoke of a future where interstellar travel was not just possible, but commonplace. A future where humans could learn from the stars, from the civilizations that had come before them.

Luna's speech was met with applause. Her words resonated with the audience, her vision for the future inspiring them. Luna was not just a colonist on an alien world; she was a visionary, a beacon of hope for the future.

And so, Luna's journey continued. She was not just a colonist on an alien world; she was a leader, a visionary, a beacon of hope. And as she stood on the stage, sharing her vision with the galaxy, she knew that her greatest achievements were yet to come.

Chapter Twenty-Seven: The Mysterious Room

The discovery of the mysterious room had been a turning point in Luna's journey. Hidden deep within the labyrinthine tunnels of an ancient ruin, the room was unlike anything they had encountered before. Its walls were covered in intricate carvings, glowing faintly with an otherworldly light, and at its center stood a pedestal holding a strange artifact.

The artifact was unlike anything Luna had seen before. It was a small, spherical object, intricately carved and glowing with the same otherworldly light as the carvings on the walls. Luna reached out to touch it, and as her fingers brushed against the cool surface of the artifact, a sudden rush of images flooded her mind.

She saw the Ancients, their civilization in its prime, their knowledge and technology far surpassing anything known to humanity. She saw their fall, the devastation that had befallen them, and the desperate measures they had taken to preserve their knowledge for future generations.

The images were overwhelming, but Luna held on, determined to understand. She saw the Ancients' final days, their desperate attempts to save their civilization, and their ultimate failure. But amidst the despair, there was hope. The Ancients had left behind their knowledge, preserved in the artifact, in the hope that someone would one day discover it and learn from their mistakes.

As the flood of images subsided, Luna was left with a profound sense of awe and responsibility. The Ancients had entrusted their legacy to whoever found the artifact, and now that responsibility fell to her. She knew that she had to share this discovery with the rest of the colony, and with the galaxy at large.

The mysterious room had revealed its secrets, but Luna knew that this was just the beginning. There was still so much to learn, so much to discover. But for now, she had a new understanding of the Ancients, and a renewed determination to honor their legacy and ensure the future of Proxima Centauri b.

Chapter Twenty-Eight: Deciphering the Alien Language

The artifact from the mysterious room had provided Luna with a wealth of information about the Ancients, but it also presented a new challenge: deciphering the alien language. The carvings on the walls and the inscriptions on the artifact were written in a language that was completely unknown to Luna and her team.

Undeterred, Luna set about the task with her usual determination. She gathered her team of linguists and historians, and together they began the painstaking process of deciphering the alien language. They started by identifying recurring symbols and patterns in the carvings and inscriptions, slowly building a rudimentary understanding of the language's structure and syntax.

As they delved deeper into the language, they began to uncover the rich history and culture of the Ancients. They learned about their beliefs, their values, and their understanding of the universe. They discovered that the Ancients were a highly advanced civilization, with a deep respect for knowledge and a strong sense of responsibility towards their planet and its ecosystem.

Deciphering the alien language was a monumental task, but Luna and her team were undeterred. They knew that the knowledge they were uncovering could have profound implications for the future of the colony and for the understanding of other civilizations in the galaxy.

With each new word they deciphered, they were one step closer to unlocking the secrets of the Ancients. And with each new discovery, Luna's resolve to honor the legacy of the Ancients and ensure the future of

Proxima Centauri b only grew stronger. The journey was far from over, but Luna was ready to face whatever challenges lay ahead.

Chapter Twenty-Nine: The History of the Ancients

With the alien language partially deciphered, Luna and her team were able to delve deeper into the history of the Ancients. The carvings on the walls of the mysterious room and the inscriptions on the artifact painted a vivid picture of a civilization that was both advanced and deeply connected to their planet.

The Ancients had a profound understanding of the universe and their place within it. They had developed technologies that were far beyond anything Luna and her team had ever seen, harnessing the power of their planet's resources without causing harm to its ecosystem.

However, the history of the Ancients was not without its dark periods. Luna's team discovered evidence of a great calamity that had befallen the civilization. It seemed that despite their advanced technology and knowledge, the Ancients were unable to prevent their own downfall.

The cause of this downfall was unclear, but the effects were evident in the ruins that Luna and her team were exploring. The once-thriving civilization had been reduced to ruins, and the Ancients themselves had disappeared, leaving behind only their knowledge and their warnings for future generations.

This discovery was a sobering reminder for Luna and her team. Despite their own advancements and achievements, they were not immune to the same fate that had befallen the Ancients. They resolved to learn from the history of the Ancients and to use their knowledge to ensure a bright future for the colony on Proxima Centauri b.

Chapter Thirty: The Fall of the Ancient Civilization

The fall of the Ancient civilization was a mystery that Luna and her team were determined to unravel. Despite their advanced technology and deep understanding of the universe, the Ancients had been unable to prevent their downfall. The ruins that Luna and her team were exploring were a stark reminder of this once-thriving civilization's fate.

Chapter Thirty-One: Lessons from the Past

The history of the Ancients served as a cautionary tale for Luna and the colony. They learned that advancement and knowledge were not enough to prevent downfall. They needed to understand and respect the delicate balance of their ecosystem and avoid the mistakes that led to the fall of the Ancients.

Chapter Thirty-Two: Changes in the Colony

Inspired by the lessons from the Ancients, changes were implemented in the colony. Sustainable practices were introduced, and efforts were made to preserve the ecosystem of Proxima Centauri b. The colony began to transform, reflecting the influence of Luna's discoveries and the lessons learned from the Ancients.

Chapter Thirty-Three: Sustainable Practices

Sustainable practices became the norm in the colony. Resources were used judiciously, waste was minimized, and renewable energy sources were utilized. The colony thrived, not at the expense of the planet, but in harmony with it. Luna's influence was evident in these changes, reflecting her commitment to preserving the legacy of the Ancients and ensuring a sustainable future for Proxima Centauri b.

Chapter Thirty-Four: Preserving the Ecosystem

Preserving the ecosystem of Proxima Centauri b became a top priority for Luna and the colony. They implemented measures to protect the planet's biodiversity and natural resources. This included careful management of water and energy resources, minimizing waste, and promoting biodiversity.

Luna and her team also worked on rehabilitating areas that had been affected by the colony's activities. They planted native flora and created habitats for the local fauna, helping to restore the balance of the ecosystem.

The preservation efforts were not just limited to the physical environment. Luna understood that the cultural and historical heritage of the Ancients was an integral part of the planet's ecosystem. She made it a point to preserve and respect the ruins and artifacts of the Ancients, ensuring they were studied and understood without causing them harm.

Through these efforts, Luna and the colony demonstrated their commitment to preserving the ecosystem of Proxima Centauri b. They understood that their survival and prosperity were intrinsically linked to the health of the planet. And they were determined to ensure that the mistakes of the Ancients would not be repeated.

Chapter Thirty-Five: Luna's Continued Explorations

Despite the many changes and advancements in the colony, Luna's thirst for exploration and discovery remained undiminished. She continued her explorations of Proxima Centauri b, venturing into uncharted territories and uncovering new mysteries.

Each expedition brought with it a wealth of knowledge about the planet and its history. Luna and her team discovered new species of flora and fauna, unearthed ancient artifacts, and found evidence of geological phenomena that offered insights into the planet's past.

But Luna's explorations were not just about discovery. They were also about understanding and preserving the delicate balance of the planet's ecosystem. She made sure that each expedition was conducted with the utmost respect for the environment and the heritage of the Ancients.

Luna's continued explorations were a testament to her enduring curiosity and her commitment to the future of Proxima Centauri b. They served as a reminder of the importance of exploration and discovery in advancing knowledge and fostering a deeper understanding of our place in the universe.

Chapter Thirty-Six: New Discoveries

Luna's continued explorations led to a series of new discoveries that further deepened their understanding of Proxima Centauri b. Each new species of flora and fauna, each unearthed artifact, and each geological phenomenon added a new piece to the puzzle.

One of the most significant discoveries was a series of ancient murals depicting the Ancients' understanding of the cosmos. These murals, found deep within a previously unexplored cave system, offered a glimpse into the Ancients' knowledge of astronomy and their place in the universe.

Another exciting discovery was a new species of bioluminescent flora. This plant, which Luna's team named "Stella Luminosa," emitted a soft, ethereal glow during the planet's long night cycles, providing a natural source of light.

Each new discovery brought with it a sense of excitement and wonder, reminding Luna and her team of the vast potential for knowledge and understanding that still lay unexplored on Proxima Centauri b. These discoveries fueled their determination to continue their explorations and to uncover the secrets that the planet still held.

Chapter Thirty-Seven: Luna's Growing Influence

As Luna's discoveries continued to reshape life on Proxima Centauri b, her influence within the colony grew. She was not just a researcher and explorer now, but a leader whose decisions impacted the entire colony.

Her commitment to sustainable practices and preservation of the ecosystem earned her respect and admiration. The changes she implemented were not always easy, but they were necessary for the long-term survival of the colony. Luna's leadership was characterized by her ability to make tough decisions in the face of adversity.

But Luna's influence extended beyond the confines of the colony. Her discoveries and research were shared with the scientific community across the galaxy, contributing to a broader understanding of alien civilizations and ecosystems. Her work inspired others to look beyond their own planets and consider the wider universe.

Luna's growing influence was a testament to her dedication, curiosity, and leadership. She had become a symbol of exploration and discovery, inspiring others to push the boundaries of knowledge and understanding. As Luna's journey continued, her influence was set to grow even further, shaping the future of Proxima Centauri b and beyond.

Chapter Thirty-Eight: Inspiring Others

Luna's journey was not just about exploration and discovery. It was also about inspiring others. Her courage in the face of the unknown, her determination to overcome challenges, and her unwavering commitment to preserving the ecosystem of Proxima Centauri b served as an inspiration to the entire colony.

Her influence extended beyond the confines of the colony. The scientific community across the galaxy followed her research and discoveries with great interest. Her work sparked curiosity and inspired a new generation of explorers and scientists.

But perhaps the most significant impact Luna had was on the younger generation in the colony. They grew up hearing stories of Luna's explorations, her discoveries, and her dedication to preserving their new home. Luna's journey inspired them to dream, to explore, and to respect the delicate balance of their ecosystem.

Luna had become more than just a researcher or an explorer. She was a role model, an inspiration, and a beacon of hope for the future. Her journey served as a reminder of the power of curiosity, the importance of respect for nature, and the limitless potential of the human spirit.

Chapter Thirty-Nine: The Power of Curiosity

Luna's journey on Proxima Centauri b was a testament to the power of curiosity. Her insatiable desire to learn and explore was the driving force behind her many discoveries and advancements in the colony.

Her curiosity led her to the mysterious room, the alien language, and the history of the Ancients. It pushed her to venture into uncharted territories, to question the known, and to seek answers to the unknown.

But Luna's curiosity was not just about seeking new knowledge. It was also about applying that knowledge for the betterment of the colony. Her curiosity led to sustainable practices, preservation of the ecosystem, and improvements in the quality of life in the colony.

The power of Luna's curiosity was felt not just in the colony, but across the galaxy. Her discoveries and research sparked curiosity in others, inspiring a new generation of explorers and scientists.

Luna's story was a reminder that curiosity is not just about asking questions, but about seeking answers. It's about pushing boundaries, challenging the status quo, and constantly striving for a deeper understanding of the world around us. As Luna's journey continued, her curiosity remained as strong as ever, propelling her towards new discoveries and adventures.

Chapter Forty: Courage in the Face of the Unknown

Luna's journey was marked by numerous challenges and uncertainties. From deciphering an alien language to uncovering the history of an ancient civilization, she faced the unknown with courage and determination.

Her courage was not just about facing physical dangers. It was also about venturing into uncharted intellectual territories, challenging established ideas, and seeking answers to questions that had never been asked before.

Luna's courage inspired others in the colony. It showed them that it was okay to question, to explore, and to seek the unknown. Her courage in the face of the unknown was a beacon of hope, guiding the colony through the challenges of life on a new planet.

As Luna's journey continued, her courage remained unwavering. Each new challenge, each new discovery, only strengthened her resolve to explore, to understand, and to thrive in the face of the unknown. Luna's courage was a testament to the human spirit, a reminder of our capacity to face the unknown with curiosity, determination, and hope.

Chapter Forty-One: Determination in Overcoming Challenges

Luna's journey on Proxima Centauri b was filled with challenges. From the initial struggles of adapting to a new environment, to the complex task of deciphering an alien language, Luna faced each challenge with unwavering determination.

Her determination was not just about overcoming physical challenges. It was also about intellectual perseverance. Luna was determined to understand the Ancients, to learn from their history, and to apply their knowledge for the betterment of the colony.

Luna's determination was infectious. It inspired others in the colony to face their own challenges with the same resolve. It fostered a culture of perseverance and resilience, qualities that were essential for the survival and growth of the colony.

As Luna's journey continued, her determination remained as strong as ever. Each new challenge was an opportunity to learn, to grow, and to push the boundaries of what was possible. Luna's determination was a testament to the power of the human spirit, a reminder that with perseverance and resolve, there is no challenge too great to overcome.

Chapter Forty-Two: The Impact of Luna's Journey

The impact of Luna's journey was far-reaching. Her discoveries and research reshaped the understanding of Proxima Centauri b, not just within the colony, but across the galaxy. The knowledge she uncovered about the Ancients and their civilization offered invaluable insights into the history of the galaxy and the potential for life on other planets.

Luna's journey also had a profound impact on the colony itself. Her commitment to sustainable practices and preservation of the ecosystem led to significant changes in the way the colony operated. These changes ensured the long-term survival of the colony and the preservation of Proxima Centauri b's unique ecosystem.

But perhaps the most significant impact of Luna's journey was the inspiration it provided. Her courage, determination, and curiosity inspired others in the colony and beyond. She showed that with perseverance and a spirit of exploration, it was possible to overcome challenges, make groundbreaking discoveries, and pave the way for a brighter future.

As Luna's journey continued, her impact continued to be felt. Each new discovery, each challenge overcome, and each step forward in the preservation of Proxima Centauri b's ecosystem was a testament to the enduring impact of Luna's journey. Her story was a reminder of the power of curiosity, the importance of sustainability, and the limitless potential of the human spirit.

Chapter Forty-Three: Luna's Legacy

Luna's legacy was as vast and enduring as the cosmos she explored. Her discoveries and research had not only transformed life on Proxima Centauri b, but they had also reshaped the understanding of life in the galaxy. The knowledge she had uncovered about the Ancients and their civilization offered invaluable insights into the history of the galaxy and the potential for life on other planets.

But Luna's legacy was not just about her discoveries. It was also about the values she embodied - curiosity, courage, determination, and respect for nature. These values were reflected in the sustainable practices she implemented in the colony and the preservation efforts she championed.

Luna's legacy lived on in the colony she helped build, in the scientific community that followed her research, and in the hearts of those she inspired. Her story served as a reminder of the power of curiosity, the importance of sustainability, and the limitless potential of the human spirit.

As Luna's journey continued, her legacy endured. Each new discovery, each challenge overcome, and each step forward in the preservation of Proxima Centauri b's ecosystem was a testament to Luna's enduring legacy. Her story was a beacon of hope, guiding humanity towards a brighter future in the cosmos.

Chapter Forty-Four: The Future of Proxima Centauri b

The future of Proxima Centauri b looked bright, thanks to Luna's enduring efforts. Her discoveries and research had laid a strong foundation for the colony's growth and prosperity. The sustainable practices she implemented ensured the long-term survival of the colony and the preservation of the planet's unique ecosystem.

The colony was set to expand, with plans for new expeditions and research projects. The search for other civilizations was ongoing, fueled by Luna's discoveries and the knowledge they had gained about the Ancients.

The development of new technologies was also on the horizon. These technologies, inspired by the Ancients' knowledge and Luna's research, promised to improve life in the colony and contribute to the preservation of the planet's ecosystem.

The preservation of the planet's ecosystem remained a top priority. Luna's research continued, with a focus on uncovering new artifacts, deciphering more of the alien language, and deepening their understanding of the Ancients.

The application of ancient knowledge in the advancement of the colony was a testament to Luna's vision. She believed in learning from the past to build a better future, and her approach was reflected in the colony's growth and development.

The future of Proxima Centauri b was a testament to Luna's enduring odyssey. Her journey had transformed the colony, inspired countless others, and paved the way for a bright future in the cosmos. As Luna's journey continued, the future of Proxima Centauri b looked brighter than ever.

Chapter Forty-Five: Luna's Family's New Life

Luna's family had adapted remarkably well to their new life on Proxima Centauri b. They had embraced the challenges and opportunities that came with living on a new planet, and they were thriving in their new environment.

Luna's parents, once apprehensive about the move, now marveled at the wonders of their new home. They took an active role in the colony, contributing their skills and knowledge to its growth and development.

Luna's younger siblings, inspired by her journey, were eager to follow in her footsteps. They spent their days learning about the planet, its ecosystem, and the history of the Ancients. They were growing up with a deep appreciation for exploration and discovery, values that Luna had instilled in them.

The transformation of Luna's family was a testament to their resilience and adaptability. They had embraced their new life with open hearts and minds, contributing to the colony's growth and embodying the spirit of exploration and discovery. Their story was a reminder of the power of family, the importance of adaptability, and the limitless potential of the human spirit.

Chapter Forty-Six: The Transformation of the Colony

He transformation of the colony on Proxima Centauri b was nothing short of remarkable. From a small group of explorers and scientists, it had grown into a thriving community, all thanks to Luna's leadership and vision.

The colony had become a beacon of sustainable living, with practices that ensured the preservation of the planet's unique ecosystem. Buildings were constructed with materials that minimized environmental impact, and energy was sourced from renewable sources. Waste was managed efficiently, and biodiversity was promoted.

The transformation was not just physical. The mindset of the colonists had also changed. Inspired by Luna's respect for the Ancients and their wisdom, the colonists embraced a lifestyle that valued knowledge, exploration, and harmony with nature.

Education was a priority, with children learning about the history of the Ancients, the importance of sustainability, and the wonders of exploration from a young age. The colony had become a place of learning and discovery, a testament to Luna's vision.

The transformation of the colony was a testament to Luna's leadership and the power of a shared vision. It was a reminder of what could be achieved when curiosity, respect for nature, and a commitment to sustainability were at the heart of a community's ethos. As Luna's journey continued, the transformation of the colony served as a beacon of hope for the future of Proxima Centauri b.

Chapter Forty-Seven: The Influence of Luna's Discoveries

Luna's discoveries had a profound influence on the colony and beyond. The knowledge she uncovered about the Ancients and their civilization offered invaluable insights into the history of the galaxy and the potential for life on other planets.

Her discovery of sustainable practices and the importance of preserving the ecosystem led to significant changes in the colony. These changes not only ensured the long-term survival of the colony but also served as a model for other colonies across the galaxy.

Luna's discoveries also influenced the scientific community. Her research sparked curiosity and inspired a new generation of explorers and scientists. Her work contributed to a broader understanding of alien civilizations and ecosystems.

But perhaps the most significant influence of Luna's discoveries was the hope they instilled. Her journey showed that with curiosity, courage, and determination, it was possible to overcome challenges, make groundbreaking discoveries, and pave the way for a brighter future.

As Luna's journey continued, her influence was set to grow even further, shaping the future of Proxima Centauri b and beyond. Her story was a beacon of hope, guiding humanity towards a brighter future in the cosmos.

Chapter Forty-Eight: The Expansion of the Colony

With Luna's guidance and the lessons learned from the Ancients, the colony on Proxima Centauri b began to expand. New habitats were built, each designed with sustainable practices in mind. These new areas were not just living spaces, but also hubs for research, education, and community activities.

The expansion was carried out with great care to minimize impact on the planet's ecosystem. Each new structure was built using materials that were either found on the planet or recycled from previous constructions. Energy-efficient technologies were used to power the habitats, and waste management systems were put in place to ensure that nothing was wasted.

As the colony expanded, so did its influence. Other colonies across the galaxy began to take notice of the sustainable practices implemented on Proxima Centauri b. Luna's discoveries and the colony's success became a model for sustainable living on other planets.

The expansion of the colony was a testament to Luna's vision and leadership. It showed that it was possible to grow and thrive while maintaining harmony with the environment. As the colony continued to expand, Luna's dream of a sustainable future on Proxima Centauri b was becoming a reality.

Chapter Forty-Nine: New Expeditions

As the colony expanded, so did the scope of Luna's explorations. New expeditions were launched, each one venturing further into the unexplored territories of Proxima Centauri b. These expeditions were not just about exploration, but also about understanding and preserving the delicate balance of the planet's ecosystem.

Each expedition was meticulously planned, with teams of scientists, explorers, and engineers working together to ensure its success. They were equipped with the latest technology, much of it developed based on Luna's research and the knowledge gleaned from the Ancients.

The new expeditions led to a wealth of new discoveries. New species of flora and fauna were cataloged, geological phenomena were studied, and more artifacts from the Ancients were uncovered. Each discovery added to the growing body of knowledge about Proxima Centauri b and its history.

But the expeditions were not without challenges. Each new territory brought with it new dangers and uncertainties. Yet, Luna and her team faced these challenges with courage and determination, their resolve strengthened by the knowledge that they were contributing to the future of the colony and the preservation of Proxima Centauri b.

As Luna's journey continued, the new expeditions promised more discoveries, more knowledge, and more opportunities to learn and grow. They were a testament to Luna's vision, her leadership, and her unwavering commitment to exploration and discovery.

Chapter Fifty: The Search for Other Civilizations

With the colony established and thriving, Luna turned her attention to the stars. The knowledge they had gained from the Ancients had sparked a curiosity about other civilizations that might exist in the galaxy.

New expeditions were launched, not just within the boundaries of Proxima Centauri b, but also into the vast expanse of space. These expeditions were equipped with advanced technology developed in the colony, much of it inspired by the Ancients' knowledge.

The search for other civilizations was a daunting task, but Luna and her team were undeterred. They knew that the potential rewards - new knowledge, new technologies, perhaps even new allies - were worth the effort.

As the search continued, Luna couldn't help but wonder what they might find. Would they discover civilizations like the Ancients, or would they encounter beings beyond their wildest imagination? The possibilities were endless, and the anticipation was thrilling.

As Luna's journey continued, the search for other civilizations became a new chapter in her enduring odyssey. It was a testament to her vision, her leadership, and her unwavering commitment to exploration and discovery. As Luna looked to the stars, the future of Proxima Centauri b, and indeed the entire galaxy, seemed brighter than ever.

Chapter Fifty-One: The Growth of Interstellar Relations

As the search for other civilizations continued, the colony on Proxima Centauri b began to play a crucial role in the growth of interstellar relations. Luna's discoveries and the knowledge gleaned from the Ancients had sparked interest across the galaxy, leading to increased communication and collaboration between different civilizations.

The colony became a hub for interstellar diplomacy and exchange of knowledge. Scientists, explorers, and diplomats from different parts of the galaxy visited the colony, eager to learn about Luna's discoveries and the sustainable practices implemented in the colony.

Luna and her team welcomed these interstellar visitors, seeing it as an opportunity to learn and share knowledge. They organized conferences, workshops, and cultural exchange programs, fostering a spirit of cooperation and mutual respect.

The growth of interstellar relations brought new opportunities and challenges. But Luna was confident that with open communication, mutual respect, and a shared commitment to sustainability, they could navigate these challenges and build a prosperous future for all.

As Luna's journey continued, the growth of interstellar relations promised a future of cooperation and mutual growth. It was a testament to Luna's vision, her leadership, and her unwavering commitment to exploration and discovery. As Luna looked to the stars, the future of Proxima Centauri b, and indeed the entire galaxy, seemed brighter than ever.

Chapter Fifty-Two: The Development of New Technologies

With the growth of interstellar relations and the continuous exploration of Proxima Centauri b, the development of new technologies became a priority for the colony. These technologies were inspired by Luna's discoveries, the knowledge gleaned from the Ancients, and the shared knowledge from other civilizations.

The new technologies ranged from advanced communication systems that facilitated interstellar dialogue, to innovative energy solutions that harnessed the unique resources of Proxima Centauri b. There were also significant advancements in the fields of agriculture, medicine, and transportation, all aimed at improving life in the colony and preserving the planet's ecosystem.

Luna and her team played a crucial role in this technological revolution. They not only provided the inspiration and knowledge for these advancements but also ensured that each technology adhered to the principles of sustainability and respect for nature.

The development of new technologies brought about significant changes in the colony. Life became more comfortable, the work more efficient, and the dream of a sustainable future on Proxima Centauri b more attainable.

As Luna's journey continued, the development of new technologies promised a future of innovation and growth. It was a testament to Luna's vision, her leadership, and her unwavering commitment to exploration and discovery. As Luna looked to the stars, the future of Proxima Centauri b, and indeed the entire galaxy, seemed brighter than ever.

Chapter Fifty-Three: The Improvement of Life in the Colony

With the development of new technologies and the expansion of the colony, life on Proxima Centauri b improved significantly. The advancements in agriculture led to an abundance of food, while improvements in medicine resulted in better healthcare for the colonists.

The new communication systems facilitated seamless interaction within the colony and with other civilizations, fostering a sense of community and mutual understanding. The innovative energy solutions not only powered the colony efficiently but also minimized their impact on the planet's ecosystem.

Education thrived in the colony, with children and adults alike having access to a wealth of knowledge about the Ancients, the history of Proxima Centauri b, and the wider universe. This culture of learning and curiosity was a testament to Luna's influence and her commitment to knowledge and discovery.

The improved transportation systems made exploration and travel within the colony and its surroundings easier and safer. This allowed for more efficient resource distribution and quicker response times in emergencies.

As Luna's journey continued, the improvement of life in the colony was a testament to her vision, her leadership, and her unwavering commitment to creating a sustainable and prosperous future on Proxima Centauri b. As Luna looked to the stars, the future of Proxima Centauri b, and indeed the entire galaxy, seemed brighter than ever.

Chapter Fifty-Four: The Preservation of the Planet's Ecosystem

The preservation of Proxima Centauri b's ecosystem was at the heart of Luna's vision for the colony. From the very beginning, Luna understood that the survival and prosperity of the colony were intrinsically linked to the health of the planet's ecosystem.

Under Luna's guidance, the colony implemented a range of measures to preserve the ecosystem. These included sustainable practices in agriculture and construction, efficient waste management systems, and the use of renewable energy sources. Luna also championed the protection of the planet's biodiversity, ensuring that the unique flora and fauna of Proxima Centauri b were preserved for future generations.

The preservation efforts extended to the cultural and historical heritage of the Ancients. Luna ensured that the ruins and artifacts of the Ancients were studied and preserved, respecting their cultural significance and learning from their wisdom.

As Luna's journey continued, the preservation of the planet's ecosystem remained a top priority. Each new discovery, each technological advancement, and each expansion of the colony was carried out with the utmost respect for the planet and its ecosystem. Luna's commitment to preservation was a testament to her vision, her leadership, and her unwavering commitment to creating a sustainable and prosperous future on Proxima Centauri b.

Chapter Fifty-Five: The Continuation of Luna's Research

Luna's research continued to be the driving force behind the colony's growth and prosperity. Her relentless pursuit of knowledge led to new discoveries, advancements in technology, and a deeper understanding of Proxima Centauri b and its history.

Her research extended beyond the confines of the colony. Luna was constantly exploring, studying the planet's unique flora and fauna, deciphering more of the alien language, and uncovering new artifacts from the Ancients. Each new discovery added to the growing body of knowledge about Proxima Centauri b and its history.

Luna's research also played a crucial role in the preservation of the planet's ecosystem. She was always looking for ways to minimize the impact of the colony on the environment, and her research often led to new sustainable practices and technologies.

As Luna's journey continued, her research remained as vibrant and dynamic as ever. Each new discovery, each challenge overcome, and each step forward in the preservation of Proxima Centauri b's ecosystem was a testament to Luna's unwavering commitment to exploration, discovery, and sustainability. As Luna looked to the stars, the future of Proxima Centauri b, and indeed the entire galaxy, seemed brighter than ever.

Chapter Fifty-Six: The Discovery of New Artifacts

As Luna's research continued, new artifacts were discovered. These artifacts, remnants of the Ancients, offered invaluable insights into their civilization and way of life. Each artifact was meticulously studied and preserved, adding to the growing body of knowledge about the Ancients.

The discovery of new artifacts was not just about understanding the past. It was also about learning lessons for the future. The Ancients had been a highly advanced civilization, yet they had fallen. Understanding their history and their mistakes could help the colony avoid a similar fate.

The discovery of new artifacts also brought with it new mysteries. Each artifact was a piece of a larger puzzle, and Luna and her team were determined to solve it. They worked tirelessly, deciphering the alien language, studying the artifacts, and piecing together the history of the Ancients.

As Luna's journey continued, the discovery of new artifacts promised more knowledge, more understanding, and more lessons for the future. It was a testament to Luna's unwavering commitment to exploration, discovery, and learning. As Luna looked to the stars, the future of Proxima Centauri b, and indeed the entire galaxy, seemed brighter than ever.

Chapter Fifty-Seven: Unraveling the Mysteries

The artifacts were like a cryptic language waiting to be deciphered, and Luna was the linguist. Each artifact was a word, and each collection of artifacts formed a sentence, narrating the tale of the Ancients. The more Luna discovered, the more fluent she became in this ancient dialect.

One day, Luna stumbled upon an artifact unlike any other. It was a device, seemingly technological in nature. It was dormant but appeared to be intact. The team speculated it could be a data storage device, a source of untapped knowledge. The excitement in the research facility was palpable.

Luna and her team worked day and night, trying to activate the device. After weeks of relentless effort, the device sprang to life. It projected a holographic display of the galaxy, with Proxima Centauri b highlighted. Symbols, presumably in the language of the Ancients, surrounded the holographic display.

The team was ecstatic. This was a breakthrough. The device was not just a storage unit; it was a map. A map that could guide them to other Ancient sites within the galaxy, perhaps even to the homeworld of the Ancients.

The discovery opened up new avenues for exploration. Luna knew this was just the beginning. The Ancients had left behind more than just artifacts; they had left behind a legacy. A legacy that Luna was determined to uncover. As she gazed at the stars, Luna knew that the future held even more discoveries, more understanding, and more lessons from the Ancients. The journey was far from over; in fact, it had just begun.

Chapter Fifty-Eight: The Path Forward

With the activation of the ancient device, Luna's mission took on a new dimension. The holographic map was a treasure trove of potential sites, each possibly holding the key to further understanding the Ancients. The team was eager to explore these locations, but they also knew the risks involved. Venturing into unknown territories could be dangerous, but the promise of discovery was too enticing to resist.

Luna decided to send probes to these locations. The probes were equipped with advanced scanning technology, capable of collecting data about the environment and any artifacts present. This would allow the team to assess the potential value of each site without risking their safety.

As the probes were dispatched, the research facility buzzed with anticipation. Each probe represented a step forward in their quest to unravel the mysteries of the Ancients. Luna knew that each piece of data could bring them closer to understanding the Ancients' civilization, their technology, and perhaps even their downfall.

Meanwhile, Luna continued to study the device. She believed that it held more secrets, more knowledge waiting to be unlocked. She was particularly intrigued by the symbols surrounding Proxima Centauri b on the holographic display. Could they be coordinates, instructions, or perhaps a warning?

As Luna delved deeper into the mysteries of the Ancients, she couldn't help but feel a sense of connection with them. They, too, had looked to the stars with curiosity and wonder. And though their civilization had fallen, their legacy lived on, guiding Luna and her team towards a future filled with discovery and understanding.

The path forward was uncertain and fraught with challenges. But Luna was undeterred. She knew that every step, every discovery, brought them closer to understanding the Ancients and ensuring the survival of their own civilization. The journey was just beginning, and Luna was ready to face whatever lay ahead.

Chapter Fifty-Nine: The First Probe Returns

The first probe had been dispatched to a location that was relatively close by, in galactic terms. After weeks of waiting, the data from the probe finally started streaming in. The research facility was abuzz with excitement as the first images were displayed.

The site was a desolate landscape, filled with the ruins of what once might have been a bustling city. Amidst the ruins, the probe had detected several artifacts. The images of these artifacts were transmitted back to the research facility, where Luna and her team began the process of analysis.

Each artifact was unique, yet they all bore the unmistakable mark of the Ancients. There were tools, seemingly used for construction and repair, devices that appeared to be communication equipment, and even what looked like a personal handheld device. These artifacts offered a glimpse into the daily lives of the Ancients.

But the most intriguing find was a large monument, standing tall amidst the ruins. The monument was adorned with symbols, similar to those found on the device. Luna speculated that this could be a memorial, a tribute to the Ancients who once thrived there.

The data from the probe was invaluable. It confirmed Luna's belief that the Ancients had spread across the galaxy, leaving behind remnants of their civilization. Each site was a chapter in the story of the Ancients, waiting to be read.

As Luna delved into the data, she couldn't help but feel a sense of awe. The Ancients had achieved so much, yet they had also lost everything. Their story was a reminder of the fragility of civilizations, no matter how advanced.

With the return of the first probe, Luna's mission had reached a significant milestone. But there was still much to be done. More probes were returning, each carrying its own set of data, its own piece of the puzzle. Luna knew that the path forward was filled with challenges, but she was ready. The story of the Ancients was waiting to be told, and Luna was determined to tell it.

Chapter Sixty: Echoes of the Past

As the data from the probes continued to pour in, Luna and her team were inundated with information. Each new site revealed more about the Ancients, their technology, their culture, and their history. The team worked tirelessly, analyzing the data, deciphering the symbols, and piecing together the story of the Ancients.

One day, while studying the data from a newly returned probe, Luna made a startling discovery. The probe had found a site with structures remarkably similar to those on Proxima Centauri b. The same symbols adorned the walls, and the layout of the city mirrored that of their own colony.

This discovery was a game-changer. It suggested that the Ancients had not just visited Proxima Centauri b, but they had lived there. They had built a city, much like the colony Luna and her team now called home.

The implications were staggering. Luna wondered, could their colony be standing on the ruins of an Ancient city? Could they be walking the same paths, living in the same buildings, looking at the same stars as the Ancients did centuries ago?

The discovery sparked a flurry of activity in the research facility. Luna ordered a thorough scan of their colony, looking for any signs of Ancient structures or artifacts. The team also started comparing the layout of their colony with the images from the probe, looking for any similarities.

As Luna delved deeper into the echoes of the past, she felt a profound connection with the Ancients. Their story was becoming her story, their history her history. The Ancients were no longer a distant civilization; they were a part of Luna, a part of her team, a part of Proxima Centauri b.

Chapter Sixty marked a turning point in Luna's mission. The Ancients were no longer just a subject of study; they were a part of their identity. As Luna gazed at the stars, she knew that their journey was far from over. The echoes of the past were guiding them towards a future filled with discovery, understanding, and a deeper connection with the Ancients.

Chapter Sixty-One: The Ancient City Beneath

The scans of their colony revealed something astonishing. Beneath the surface of Proxima Centauri b, hidden under layers of soil and rock, lay the remnants of an Ancient city. The structures were remarkably preserved, a testament to the Ancients' advanced construction techniques.

The discovery sent ripples of excitement through the research facility. Luna and her team had been living atop a treasure trove of Ancient artifacts and structures. The colony was not just a home; it was a living museum, a window into the past.

Excavation began immediately. Luna's team worked meticulously, unearthing structures and artifacts, each more intriguing than the last. There were dwellings, public spaces, and even what appeared to be a research facility, much like their own.

Among the artifacts, they found a device similar to the one that had led them to this discovery. It was damaged but still held a wealth of data. Luna speculated that this device could hold the key to understanding why the Ancients had left Proxima Centauri b and where they had gone.

As Luna and her team delved deeper into the Ancient city, they felt a profound sense of awe and respect. They were walking through the echoes of the past, touching the remnants of a civilization that had once looked to the stars, just as they were doing now.

The Ancient city beneath their colony was a constant reminder of the transience of civilizations. It was a humbling experience, but it also filled them with determination. They were not just uncovering the past; they were building their future. A future where the mistakes of the Ancients would not be repeated, where the knowledge of the past would guide them towards a sustainable and prosperous future.

Chapter Sixty-One marked a new phase in Luna's mission. The Ancient city beneath their feet was a symbol of their connection with the Ancients, a symbol of their shared history and shared future. As Luna looked to the stars, she knew that their journey was far from over. The echoes of the past were guiding them, and the future was waiting to be discovered.

Chapter Sixty-Two: The Message from the Ancients

The excavation of the Ancient city continued, revealing more about the civilization that once thrived on Proxima Centauri b. Amidst the ruins, Luna and her team discovered a central plaza with a large monument at its heart. The monument was adorned with the same symbols found on the device, and Luna felt a sense of anticipation as they approached it.

As they neared the monument, the device Luna carried began to react. It vibrated softly at first, then more intensely as they got closer. Luna held the device up to the monument, and to their astonishment, the symbols on the monument began to glow.

Suddenly, a holographic projection emerged from the monument. It was an Ancient, speaking in their language. The device immediately began to translate. The Ancient spoke of their civilization, their achievements, and their downfall. They spoke of a cataclysmic event, a disaster of their own making that led to their extinction.

The message was a warning and a plea. A warning to not repeat their mistakes, and a plea to remember them, to learn from them. The Ancients had reached for the stars, but in their hubris, they had brought about their own end.

The message from the Ancients resonated with Luna and her team. They felt a sense of responsibility, a duty to heed the Ancients' warning. They were the custodians of the Ancients' legacy, and they were determined to ensure that their civilization would not meet the same fate.

Chapter Sixty-Two was a sobering reminder of the perils of unchecked progress. But it also filled them with hope. The Ancients had entrusted them with their history, their lessons, and their hopes for the future. Luna knew that their journey was far from over. The echoes of the past were guiding them, and the future was waiting to be discovered.

Chapter Sixty-Three: A New Dawn

The message from the Ancients had a profound impact on Luna and her team. They realized that their mission was not just about exploration and discovery, but also about preservation and learning. They were the stewards of the Ancients' legacy, and they had a responsibility to ensure that their civilization did not repeat the same mistakes.

Luna decided to share the message from the Ancients with the entire colony. She believed that everyone had a right to know about their past and the lessons they needed to learn. The message was broadcasted throughout the colony, and the reaction was overwhelming. There was a sense of unity, a shared purpose that brought the colony closer together.

In the days that followed, Luna and her team continued their work with renewed vigor. They studied the Ancient city, learning more about their technology, their culture, and their downfall. They also started implementing changes in their own society, taking steps to ensure sustainability and balance.

Meanwhile, the probes continued to explore the galaxy, uncovering more Ancient sites. Each new discovery brought them closer to understanding the Ancients and their civilization. But Luna knew that their journey was far from over. There were still many mysteries to unravel, many lessons to learn.

Chapter Sixty-Three marked a new dawn for the colony. They were no longer just survivors on a distant planet; they were the bearers of a legacy, the successors of an ancient civilization. As Luna looked to the stars, she knew that their future was bright. Guided by the echoes of the past, they were ready to face whatever lay ahead. The journey of discovery, learning, and growth was just beginning.

Chapter Sixty-Four: Legacy of the Ancients

The revelation of the Ancients' history had a profound impact on the colony. Luna's decision to share the message from the Ancients led to a shift in the colony's perspective. They were not just colonists trying to survive on a distant planet; they were the inheritors of a rich and ancient legacy.

The Ancient city beneath their colony became a place of learning and reflection. Luna established a museum, where artifacts from the Ancient city were displayed. The museum was not just a place to observe; it was a place to learn, to understand, and to remember the Ancients.

Meanwhile, Luna continued her research. The device from the Ancient city was a constant source of new information. Each day brought new discoveries, new insights into the Ancients' civilization. Luna was particularly intrigued by the Ancients' understanding of the cosmos. Their knowledge was far beyond anything the colony had previously imagined.

The probes sent to other Ancient sites across the galaxy were also yielding fascinating results. Each site was unique, yet they all bore the unmistakable mark of the Ancients. The data from the probes was meticulously analyzed, adding to the growing body of knowledge about the Ancients.

Chapter Sixty-Four was a testament to the enduring legacy of the Ancients. Their civilization might have fallen, but their knowledge, their wisdom, and their warnings lived on. Luna and her team were not just uncovering the past; they were shaping the future. Guided by the echoes of the past, they were charting a course towards a future where the mistakes of the Ancients would not be repeated. The journey was far from over, and the legacy of the Ancients was just beginning to unfold.

Chapter Sixty-Five: The Dawn of a New Era

The legacy of the Ancients had become a guiding light for the colony. Their knowledge and wisdom, preserved through the artifacts and structures, were now shaping the future of Proxima Centauri b. Luna and her team were not just researchers; they were the torchbearers of an ancient civilization, carrying forward its legacy.

The museum established by Luna became a hub of learning and innovation. It was here that the colonists learned about the Ancients' advanced technology, their understanding of the cosmos, and their culture. The museum was not just a place to remember the past; it was a place to envision the future.

Meanwhile, the data from the Ancient device continued to unravel new mysteries. Luna discovered references to other civilizations, suggesting that the Ancients were not alone in the galaxy. This revelation opened up new possibilities and questions. Were these civilizations still thriving? Could they establish contact?

The probes sent across the galaxy were also making remarkable discoveries. They found Ancient sites on distant planets, each with its unique story. The data from these sites was adding to their understanding of the Ancients and their interstellar journey.

Chapter Sixty-Five marked the dawn of a new era for the colony. They were no longer just survivors on a distant planet; they were a thriving civilization, guided by the wisdom of the Ancients. The journey was far from over. With each passing day, they were getting closer to understanding their past and shaping their future. The legacy of the Ancients was living on, guiding them towards a future filled with discovery, understanding, and growth.

Afterword:

As we close the pages on this remarkable journey of Luna and her team, we are left with a profound sense of awe and respect for the Ancients, their wisdom, and their legacy. This story is not just about the discovery of an ancient civilization; it's about the lessons we learn from the past and how we apply them to our future.

The Ancients, despite their advanced knowledge and technology, fell victim to their own actions. Their story serves as a stark reminder of the consequences of unchecked progress and the importance of balance and sustainability. It's a lesson that Luna and her team took to heart, shaping their own society to avoid the same fate.

But this story is also about hope and the unquenchable human spirit of exploration and discovery. Luna's journey is a testament to our innate curiosity and our relentless pursuit of knowledge. It's a celebration of our ability to look beyond our own world, to reach for the stars, and to seek answers to the mysteries of the universe.

As we look forward to the next chapters of Luna's journey, we are reminded that we are not alone in this vast cosmos. The echoes of the Ancients guide us, their wisdom shapes us, and their legacy lives on in us. We are the torchbearers of their knowledge, the stewards of their legacy, and the architects of our future.

In the end, this is not just Luna's story; it's our story. It's a story of our past, our present, and our future. It's a story of our place in the cosmos and our journey towards understanding and growth. As we move forward, guided by the echoes of the past, we step into a future filled with promise and potential.

Here's to the journey ahead.

Don't miss out!

Visit the website below and you can sign up to receive emails whenever Tiffany Tunis publishes a new book. There's no charge and no obligation.

https://books2read.com/r/B-A-TASBB-ULERC

www.ingramcontent.com/pod-product-compliance
Lightning Source LLC
Chambersburg PA
CBHW061348140726
47997CB00003B/1110